Lifesong

Julia Blake

To keit
Best wishes
Julia Blake

Sele Books
www.selebooks.com

www.juliablakeauthor.co.uk

ISBN: 9781986466813

Lifesong is written in British English,
Estimated UK film rating of this book: 12+
with mild sexual references.

Lifesong is an Authors Alike
accredited book.

~ Dedication ~

To all who struggle to save
us from ourselves and to
make a difference

~ Acknowledgements ~

A big thank you, as ever to my wonderful editor Dani. Thanks, missy, you are a stern taskmaster, but I wouldn't have you any other way.

Thanks, must also go to James and Becky Wright at Platform House Publishing for all their patient help with formatting and all their advice and creative input with the cover and interior graphics. Thanks, guys, you are amazing.

For all your publishing needs, contact Becky at:-

www.platformhousepublishing.co.uk

Finally, a big thank you to my daughter for all her help with illustrations and all the technical bits that I didn't understand.

~ A Note for the Reader ~

I have always been passionate about the environment and am deeply concerned about the direction we, as a species, are going as landlords of this glorious planet.

Back in 2006, I was also very fond of the music of Karl Jenkins – especially his Adiemus album – which explored the range of sounds the human voice can make without using actual words. Combined with my lifelong appreciation of science fiction, Lifesong was a natural offspring of those loves.

I entered Lifesong in the L. Ron Hubbard – Writers of the Future Novella Competition. To my delight, it was very highly placed and that inspired me to continue writing.

Then in 2017 I decided to become an indie author and published Lifesong first as an eBook, then as a paperback the following year. So far, it has received nothing but critical acclaim.

You can find out more about me, my books, and my crazy life at:

Website: www.juliablakeauthor.co.uk
Facebook: Julia Blake Author
Instagram: @juliablakeauthor
Blog: https://juliablakeauthor.home.blog

~ Table of Contents ~

Copyright
Dedication
Acknowledgements
A Note for the Reader
"Music of the Spheres"

About the Author
A Note from Julia
Other Books by the Author

~ Music of the Spheres ~

For many centuries, the ancients believed in something they called **Musica Universalis** (literally universal music), also called Music of the Spheres or Harmony of the Spheres. This was a philosophical concept that regards the movement of celestial bodies – the Sun, Moon and Planets – as a form of musica (the medieval Latin term for music).

This "music" is not thought to be literally audible, but a harmonic, mathematical or religious concept. The idea continued to appeal to thinkers about music until the end of the Renaissance.

Lifesong

Julia Blake

Chapter One
The Grieving

It was a glorious night for his passing on. As the twin moons rose and darkness fell, she reflected on how perfect it all was. He would have loved the beauty of this night and appreciated the rightness of the traditional ritual. He would have taken comfort from it. Except, he was not here, and it was left to her to take comfort where she could.

So many had gathered to send him on his way – many faces she knew, many unfamiliar. It did not surprise her. Her grandsire had been well known for the generosity of his heart and the wisdom of his words, dispensing one as freely as the other.

Taking a deep breath, she adjusted her cloak and stepped lightly onto the path. It must begin.

She must be the one to start it. At her approach, the singing, which had been low, muted, and harmonious, rose in volume. It gloried and soared, as the singers' voices skilfully twisted the strands of what had been his life and offered it to all as a benediction.

Slowly she paced until she reached the apex of the rise, and saw the group of elders who awaited her, flaming torches in hand. Their lifesong flowed from them in wise, measured notes, and their faces were dignified with the sagacity of their age.

She bowed in acknowledgement of their status. Taking a torch from them, she felt the heat on her face, its sparks dazzling her eyes until the darkness beyond glittered in reflection.

Leaving them, she crested the hill and saw the pyre waiting, her grandsire's body wrapped in its ceremonial robes. Two council members stopped her, staffs crossed to bar her path, demanding to know her business. In accordance with custom, she sang of her grandsire, of his life, his death, and of her duty as his much-beloved grandchild, to send his lifesong on its final journey into the heavens to join the universal great song.

They bent their heads in recognition of her right, lowering their staffs until the points crossed on the ground before her. Carefully, holding the torch aloft, she stepped over them and walked to the pyre.

She waited, head bowed in acknowledgement of the solemnity of the moment and the perfection of the rites until the funeral song had reached its pinnacle and it was time to play her part. Softly at first, then gaining in ascendancy, she wove her notes into the whole. Joyfully she offered her thanks for his presence in her life, singing of the many kindnesses her grandsire had shown her, and his talent for songsculpting, which he had passed on to her.

Briefly, she touched on the superficial sorrow that he was no longer there to guide her, then let her throat open in sublime knowledge of the new song he was now part of. That great, all-encompassing song, which wove and twisted throughout existence, sweeping up all before it into one immense, perfect, never-ending, constantly harmonious stream of sound. Finally, moments or hours later, the singers stopped; the funeral song ended. The final flawless note echoed into ringing silence, and all joined for a moment in still contemplation.

Then she stepped forward and thrust the burning brand deep into the heart of the pyre.

Much later, long after the ceremony had finally ended and all had departed, she was alone in their dwelling place. The liquid perfection of the dawn lulled her, and she sat on the doorstep, the entrance to the dwelling and her heart open to absorb the last drops of sunrise.

She sang, softly and without purpose, a gently lilting melody. It touched on the awareness of her lifesong and how it must now be adjusted. The hole created by her grandsire's passing needed to be smoothed over. She understood that he was not gone, that he had merely passed on to a new place, a better place, where life eternal flowed through the stars and planets. Yet … he had gone. He was not here with her. She was alone.

Crossly, she told herself this was not so. How could she be alone with so many others for companionship? When if she so chose, she could spend time with friends and neighbours. When her workshop always hummed with the busyness of those come to barter their goods for her much sought-after sculptures.

No, she was not alone. Yet … she was lonely.

There was a disturbance in the undergrowth, a tiny squeak. With her heightened senses, she felt the demise of a small creature, the abrupt cessation of its lifesong. An instant later, Lani, her cat, stepped forward, a tiny creature dangling from her jaws.

Trotting past, Lani angled her head to look up, ears flattening as if warning her to try and deny her this prize. She smiled at the cat's antics, feeling sorry for the rodent's demise, yet amused by the smugness of the cat's lifesong which settled into a happy, rumbling purr, as she crouched and crunched on tiny bones.

Distracted, her song ended. She tilted her head to survey the flaming sky, awed and humbled by its eternal majesty.

Her grandsire had enjoyed contemplating the heavens, theorising on the life that possibly existed on those far away worlds. Often, the discussion had led to a gentle debate as he placed before her new and alarming ideas.

Perhaps the lifesong of their occupants might be very different from their own. Maybe, he even suggested – and she had shuddered with horror at the very thought - there was no lifesong on those glimmering distant specks of light.

Here, the agreement had parted. She could not conceive of a world without lifesong. Of a world whose occupants existed in silence, bereft of the music which shaped reality. How could such beings survive without becoming insane? Even the simplest of animals recognised the natural harmony of life.

An ant – carrying a leaf back to his colony, danced to the music of his race, his lifesong busy and ordered. Birds – glorying in the freedom of the skies, their lifesong erupting in wildly spontaneous notes of purest sound – all embodied the very essence of the great song which embraced and surrounded all.

She argued that the humblest single-celled being, to the more complex and emotive animals such as themselves, all paced their allotted lifespan to their individual lifesong. To not sing, to not even be aware of the great song ... such a thing was impossible.

Her grandsire had laughed at her discomfort, softly singing words of ease and reconciliation, until she had smiled again, dismissing his wild ideas as the stuff of childish nightmares. Impossible and inconceivable, and yet...

She shifted uncomfortably on the hard wooden step, remembering occasions when she had not been allowed to know his thoughts. Those times when the elders came, and they were closeted for long sessions within her grandsire's private chamber. During these visits, she attempted to keep busy by creating, but her song had been distracted and disjointed with bizarre impressions of what was occurring behind the firmly closed door. She knew these frequent meetings with the elders to be a great honour for her grandsire, but still, she was resentful for not being included.

After the elders had taken their leave with words and music of dignified thanks, he would look at her work. Brow creasing, tutting with displeasure at the awkward jaggedness of their outline, his eyes would rest thoughtfully on her, and she would know he was aware of her unease, perhaps even understanding the source of those dark and unconnected thoughts which so distorted her sculptures.

And now he was gone. She was alone in the gathering bloom of the day, gazing at the heavens which had engendered such lively debate. Her loss at his passing swelled in her breast and she gave words to her grief, gaining comfort in their shape and form. Her song culminated in a long, perfect note that soared upwards, reaching, straining until suddenly she was amongst the stars looking down on the spinning beauty of her planet.

Startled and frightened, heart pounding within her chest, she snapped back to reality, thrilled with the exciting realisation that she had travelled further than ever before. Perhaps further than anyone had ever travelled before.

Eventually, her words dwindled to a low, background hum, in perfect pitch to the beating of her heart and the rushing of the blood in her veins. Drowsily, her lids fell over eyes wearied from the ceremony and the singing of her grandsire's lifesong – the acknowledgement of his existence. The flames of his funeral pyre still leapt in her memory, twisting, and rising, a column of flames stretching to the sky, carrying his lifesong ever upwards. Her thoughts slipped free from their mooring within her mind, roaming, seeking, questioning...

A place ... other...

Heat ... intense and melting...

Terror ... stark and immobilising...

Its taste sickened in her mouth. The blaze roared like a wild beast, consuming what looked to be some sort of dwelling in front of her. It seemed – impossible as it was – that she was inside another's thoughts and emotions. That she viewed through the eyes of another, eyes raw from smoke and the angry, frustrated tears of horrified shock.

She heard strange words issuing from her host's throat, words wrenched from a throat sand dry and hoarse from screaming. She felt the restraint of others, knowing the body she looked from to be held fast in the tight grip of two beings.

She also felt the angry twisting as it fought to free itself … struggling to break away. Further, she knew should the being succeed, it aimed to plunge headlong into the inferno...

Her eyes opened. Brilliant sunlight dazzled overhead, her senses pulsing to the sounds of the morning, and the steady pace of her lifesong, her heart beating in tune with its rhythm.

Where had she been?

What had she been?

Behind her eyelids, she still saw the bright hunger of the flames, and feel the voraciousness of its appetite as it gobbled and consumed. Deep within, she could still emote to the wildly throbbing sting of bitter despair, experiencing again the overwhelming loss and pain of the strange being, whose mind and thoughts she had so briefly inhabited...

Chapter Two
The Flames

Distracted, anxious, and lacking an appetite, she silently assembled a simple breakfast, aware that after the ritualistic fasting in preparation for the funeral ceremony, sustenance of some description was required.

The food was a stabilising influence on her body. She sensed nutrients being absorbed from the berries and nuts she had consumed but tasted nothing, her mind so shaped by the events of the night, and the strange vision she had been granted.

She slept fitfully. Again, and again, her thoughts returned to the being she had briefly shared consciousness with, weeping silent tears of sympathy at his loss and anger.

She wondered at her surety that it had been male, but somehow knew that raw, frustrated grief had been masculine in its intensity.

For many days after, her lifesong was disturbed and disordered, and she struggled with unquiet disharmony to attain that level of placid contentment she was accustomed to in her life and work.

Over and over, she would sternly instruct herself to desist from such thoughts. It had been a mere nightmare, a shade brought on by lack of food, the stresses of the funeral, and natural grief at the loss of her grandsire, its substance dictated by memories of their frequent debates.

Looked at logically, the vision could be explained away quite easily. Yet she remembered all too vividly the sting of the flames, the throb of the other being's heart, the ache of his pain and the violence of his frustrated rage, to dismiss it as merely a vision caused by an empty stomach.

She attempted to lose herself in work but found her songsculptures took on a life of their own. Whatever medium she chose – be it wood or stone – the natural lifesong she felt deep within the material changed upon completion into great flames, licking and caressing, desiring to consume all in its path.

She blamed the lifesong already present within the pieces but knew the fault to be hers. It was her lifesong moulding them, causing them to take on the shape of her nightmare.

Finally, she laid her work aside, accepting that this period of mourning and adjustment was more protracted and powerful than she had previously imagined. And until it had ebbed, nothing was to be gained from attempting normality.

She escaped down the narrow cliff path to the beach, her forever refuge, where fierce winds sang loudly, and crashing surf beat frenzied time. Slipping off her clothes, she plunged naked into the starkly freezing waves.

The sea fought like a wild animal to claim her, buffeting her with icy cold fists of water. She threw her head back, exulting in the music of its cruelly magnificent strength. She fought against its grip with all her might, thrilling as her body hummed with the sheer exhilaration of the battle.

At last, she staggered to shore, spent yet refreshed, and hastily rubbed life into a body numbed from cold, pulling on clothes before falling to the sand in total abandonment, her lifesong pulsing in every cell.

Her grandsire had been fearful every time she went to the sea, and she had understood his concerns. She was too young to remember the day her parents went out on its waves and did not return but knew the memory of that time was etched within his heart forever. Strong arms and soft voices, vague memories of laughter and loving embraces, were all the remembrances she carried of her parents.

Yet, her grandsire had raised her true, awakening skills which lay dormant within her until the day she sang her first songsculpture into existence.

Proudly, she ran to show him the image she had created, feeling the connection to her lifesong, and understanding that her choice had been made.

She was to be a songsculptor as her parents had been before her, and her grandsire before them.

The sand was hot beneath her spine, and she arched her body skywards, offering herself up to the sun, her mind blank and unfocused...

... and it took her as speedily as it had before.

Her eyes opened in another's head. Looking, seeing, yet not understanding. A place ... a room unlike any she had ever seen before. Hard, rectangular lines of furniture, lit by a source she could not comprehend, illuminating with no visible means of energy.

No candle or oil lamp ever burnt with such a hard, steady light in her world, and her eyes winced away from its harshness.

Once again, she was a traveller within a host. Was it the same one? Her instincts told her it was, and she became aware of the being, sitting slumped in a kind of chair, its shiny, unforgiving black surface moving as he leant forward and rested his head in his hands.

She felt the pressure of skin on his forehead as he rubbed and felt the answering throb of pain in his skull. She understood the ache but was separate from it – a mere passenger within his mind.

He sat in fearful solitude. In the silence of aloneness, he felt himself slipping back to the point when he had lost everything to the flames.

They licked at his being, keeping him prisoner in that moment, not allowing the agony to ever cease. He cried out, flailing with an uncoordinated hand, sending a glass crashing to the floor.

His pain and anguish were so raw, so immediate, that she cowered away from its sharp edges, crawling to the furthest corners of his mind, curling up as small as she could make herself…

… and opened her eyes to the brilliance of the sun, her thoughts a confusion of emotions, struggling to understand what had occurred, her lifesong pulsing in sympathy to the pain of another.

Sleep was elusive that night. In vain she closed her eyes in the darkness, willing the gentle oblivion of slumber to claim her, only for thoughts and images to crowd behind her lids demanding attention.

Finally, she ceased trying and rolled onto her back. Tentatively, fearfully, she cleared her mind of all thought, reached out and waited…

Prepared for it this time, the transition was smoother, less shocking. Once again, she felt herself to be within the confines of the being's mind and saw the darkness of thought where the flames still lived.

He murmured something incomprehensible, and she understood him to be gripped in the sleep of sheer exhaustion, the bedclothes crumpled and soaked, as his body twitched and fretted at torturous memories.

Desperately, she sought for his lifesong, attempting to comfort and soothe him, to sing with him notes of calming sympathy. With rising panic, she reached deeper for his lifesong … and found blankness, a void, nothing.

He had no lifesong!

The absolute shock of it made her cry out in horror, shrinking away from such an aberration, fearfully groping for her lifesong.

Relief drenched her as she caught hold of its familiar rhythm, using its time and pace to quieten his racing heart, to calm the blood rushing through his veins.

He awoke with a speed which startled, his body catapulting upright, a hoarse yell echoing off sterile white walls.

Suddenly, she was aware of his conscious mind, probing, questioning. He seemed aware of her ... could feel her mind crouched within his, the song still quivering through his brain.

He arose from the bed and paced catlike across the floor, taking her with him into a smaller room. From its furnishings, she guessed it to be where he performed his ablutions but never had she imagined such things.

He pulled at a cord hanging from the ceiling. Instantly, bright draining light flooded the room, hurting her eyes. She blinked and felt his lids close, realising that she could influence his movements, to a degree.

He ran water into a basin from some sleek, shining device, splashed it onto his face, and she felt its chill, its wetness, and then the softness of the towel he used to dry himself.

He raised his head and stared into the oversized mirror on the wall, and she stared back at him, seeing him for the first time. Not so different from the men of her world, she thought, though paler of skin.

He leant closer to the mirror examining his face and she felt shocked at his eyes of vivid blue, contrasting them in her mind with the topaz-coloured eyes of her people.

He moaned, touching the cool glass with his hot forehead. Again, she felt pity well at his pain, singing softly to him words of love and hope.

Who are you?

His snapped words threw her backwards. Somehow, it was as if she was free of his mind, and that she now stood behind him, looking over his shoulder at his reflection in the mirror. Their eyes seemed to meet in the glass, and she saw the frown which tugged at his brow.

This is crazy, I'm going crazy, I thought, could have sworn...

He shook his head, his confusion plain, and she reached out and touched him.

Lilith?

The name was thrown despairingly at her, yet she knew from the directionless focus of his gaze, that he could not see her as she saw him. He collapsed to the floor in bitter anguish...

... and she awoke in her solitary bed, tasting the salt of her tears...

Chapter Three
The Sharing

H er thoughts returned to him constantly during the days which followed. But she tried to keep her mind occupied and did not seek to attain that state of thoughtlessness that seemed to herald the transition to his mind. Deliberately so, as it had confused and frightened her, the experience of being so entrenched within another's mind, witness to his all-consuming rage and grief.

She wondered about him all the time – who he was, and what tragedy had befallen him to render him so bereft and alone.

Instinctively, she felt it to be connected to the fire she had witnessed, remembering his desperate struggle to free himself from those who held him back.

She thought about the name he had cried out with such tormented hope it had torn at her heart.

Lilith.

Who was Lilith?

Perhaps his mate? Perhaps it was her loss he mourned.

She tried to imagine losing a loved one and not having the comfort of knowing they were now part of the great song – of feeling their presence moving through your lifesong.

She shuddered, tasting the rank tang of bile in her throat at the thought. How would one survive such a complete and utter loss without going mad?

Finally, alone in her bed one night, she did what she had known all along she would do. She cleared her mind, and returned to him…

He was alone again, sitting at a table. It took her a moment to realise that this time she had not returned to her customary position within his thoughts.

Instead, she was apart from his body, standing behind him, watching, trying to understand his movements as his fingers flew swiftly over some manner of device.

Flat and sleek, made of a shining substance she could not distinguish – not wood or stone – it was like nothing she had ever encountered before, and she craned her neck curiously over his shoulder.

The length of her forearm, the device seemed to be made of two halves, with one half lying flat on the table. His fingers tapped industriously at the small buttons which were positioned on this half, and she saw they all carried strange, meaningless markings.

The other half of the device was folded up at an angle, brightly glowing with a strange white light, and matching symbols to those on the lower portion appeared on it as his fingers moved. She watched and saw how his eyes never left it, as though it was imparting knowledge of immense importance.

Tentatively, she felt for its lifesong, yet there was nothing. Whatever this device, it was not natural.

Curiously, she looked around, realising they were outside on some sort of balcony. To her right was a massive window, and through it, she could make out the room she had visited previously.

She turned to her left and felt her heart almost stop with wonderment. They were high, so high above the ground it made the cliffs overlooking her shore paltry by comparison, and spread out before her, were ranks and tiers of what she assumed to be other dwellings, stacked on top of one another, jammed close, no space between them.

Her eyes grew wide at the sight. They were so numerous! Never had she seen so many dwellings clustered together in one site. On her world, although some families did construct their dwellings close to one another, most people liked to maintain a distance around their homes – space to breathe, to be apart, room to feel the harmonies and rhythms of life flow through you.

But this vast forest of shining material and endless expanse of ever-higher rooftops – this was like nothing she had encountered before or ever imagined.

She turned away, discomfited, returning her attention to the man, and reaching out for him with her mind, softly placing restful notes into his thoughts, curious to learn if the flames still imprisoned him.

His fingers stilled and then stopped as if he were aware of her presence. Emboldened, she pressed deeper, unable to explain to herself this fascination he held for her.

I feel you.

His words murmured so low she barely heard them, shocked her. For a moment she paused, her thoughts still entangled with his, then moved deeper within his mind, soothing and calming, showing him her intent was peaceful, her motives those of friendliness.

Who … what are you? You feel so real, yet I know you can't be. I know this must be some sort of dream, or hallucination, but you feel so real.

I am real.

Finally, she spoke, unable to remain silent any longer, and he started in his chair, fingers flying to his temples, his eyes flicking wildly over his shoulder to look through where she stood.

How ... where are you?

Behind you. Within you. You cannot see me, but I can see you, I can feel you.

Are you a ghost?

She paused, considering his question. The concept of ghosts was not strange to her. Indeed, the lifesong of the departed which echoed softly around that of the living could perhaps be termed ghostly, but she did not believe this to be his meaning of the word.

I am not dead if that is what you mean. I live, I am, I exist.

But where?

Far away from here. In another place, another world.

How is this possible?

I do not know. I only know my lifesong has brought me to this place, and you.

Lifesong? I don't understand, what's a lifesong?

The song which flows through each, and every, living being. It binds and connects us all to life, to the universe and to the great song itself to which we all, when we die, return.

Great song? What do you mean by that?

Can you not feel it? she cried out in a sudden passion, needing to make him hear and understand.

It is all around us, flows through and over us. Are you so deaf you cannot hear it? How can your species survive without it? Without a lifesong, surely you must all go insane. It gives life meaning, a purpose. If there is no music within you, then what is the reason for existence?

He was silent, head bowed as if considering her words. Finally, when he spoke, his voice was low and empty with the bleakness of remembrance.

Perhaps you are right. Perhaps there is no meaning to life. At least, there is none left to mine.

The flames?

She felt his surprise, the sting of shock echoing through her memories.

You know about that?

I was there, I saw, yet I did not understand.
My wife, my children ...

He stopped, groaning with pain, and buried his head in his hands. She slipped from his mind, not wishing to invade his privacy or to bear witness to his pain, understanding the power of his loss.

Perhaps a loss so strong it had found an answering resonance in her grief and dragged her here, to this place, to him.

I am sorry...

She winced at the inadequacy of her words. Helplessly, she cut the connection and fled back to her world, to that which was familiar and comforting...

Fervently, she vowed she would not return – all the while knowing she was lying to herself. She could not stay away. The hold he had upon her was too strong to be ignored.

He filled her thoughts and movements. She began to work again, yet in every piece she sang into creation, she saw his face – the shape of his hands, the line of his jaw, the shockingly alien blue of his eyes.

People came as usual to barter their products for her highly sought-after pieces. They looked at her creations, their expressions showing confusion at such a radical change of style.

Still, they must have had the power to please and intrigue, for at the end of the day every new piece had been exchanged, and her cupboards were full of the supplies she needed.

Then she mourned. All which had been inspired by him, all she had created, was gone. She worked long into the night, singing until her voice grew weak and hoarse. Then she slept.

A dreamless, exhausted slumber, it left her body unsatisfied, fatigued, and her mind foggy with distraction…

I knew you'd come back. At least, I hoped you would. He rolled over on his bed to look at where she lay beside him in the gloom of the dimly lit room. With a thrill of realisation, she knew he saw her.

You see me now?

Yes, that is…

He stopped, frowned, and she watched the play of emotions travel across his face. Although different from the men on her world, his face was still very pleasing to look upon – at least she found it to be so.

I see something … a flicker of light, a shadow. Is that you, lying there beside me?

Yes.

She reached out, touched his cheek, and saw his eyes widen, his hand flying to his face in wonder.

Did you feel that?

I'm not sure. It felt like a whisper of breeze on a summer's day…

He stopped abruptly, plainly embarrassed, and she smiled, pleased with the imagery, glad of such proof of soul for she had wondered.

In the absence of a lifesong could this man be considered to even be alive? To even have a soul. It seemed so alien, so wrong, to reach out with her lifesong and feel nothing – no spark of resonance, no answering harmony.

What you said before, about there being no music in my world, you're wrong. We have music, lots of it, it's all around us. Here, listen.

He arose from the bed, and she felt bereft at his absence, watching curiously as he touched the front of another strange device, this one gleaming black, and sound, music, suddenly issued from it.

She listened, pleased when he returned to the bed and once more lay beside her, his face turned towards hers, watching intently the space he knew she occupied.

Hear that? Music. My world is full of music. Everywhere you go, there will be music playing.

She sighed indulgently, seeking for the words to explain without sounding as if she patronised or undermined in any way, not wishing to offend or cause him pain.

Yes, this is music, yet it is not lifesong; it is not the great song. This is superficial, surface music. My world too is full of this music, created for enjoyment and entertainment … but there is so much more. You cannot understand if you have never experienced it. A person's lifesong defines them. It gives shape to their talents. My lifesong has given me the power to create, to sculpt, and the pieces reveal their true shapes when I sing it forth from them.

She stopped, seeing from his baffled frown that he did not understand. Inhaling lightly, she reached for his mind, flooding it with lifesong, sharing its joyous harmony.

She showed him the music which filled her life, was always present, sometimes as nothing more than a background hum, sometimes a light, haunting refrain which lingered through thoughts and brushed lightly over emotions. She shared glimpses of the great song, reaching out with her lifesong, taking him with her, rolling in rhythm.

Together they touched the stars, feeling the pulse of life in their fiercely burning hearts. With a thrill of discovery, she realised she was travelling further, faster, and deeper, than ever before. Whole universes, millions of them, flashed by, insubstantial, fleeting, and through it all pulsed the great song.

Breathlessly, they landed back on the bed. Somehow on their voyage their hands had become entwined. She felt the rasp of his palm, skin against skin. Heard the hoarse sound of his breathing, unsteady and ragged as it echoed in the stillness of the room.

She turned to look at him and saw the stunned wonder in his eyes, the flush of exhilaration on his cheeks.

Slowly, as she watched, his breathing calmed, regaining its even, steady pace. His eyes became focused, their vivid blueness losing the glaze of fantasy to fix on her, on her face, her body.

I see you, he murmured, his gaze roaming over each of her features as though committing them to memory.

I see you quite clearly now, you are so beautiful. Your eyes … I have never seen eyes that colour before. I feel they could look right through me.

Your eyes also are strange to me, yet they are not displeasing.

They shared a smile, uncertain of what to say or feel. Then she felt a great wave of weariness sweep over her as if their journey amongst the cosmos had depleted her lifesong. Her eyes closed.

No, wait ... don't go!

Dimly, she heard him cry out, then...

... she awoke in her bed to find Lani pawing at her, piteously demanding breakfast. It was dawn. All around she felt the lifesong of the creatures in the forest stirring, preparing to greet the sun and the start of another day.

Chapter Four
The Visitor

*T*ell me about your world? She did not answer him immediately, staring at the joining of their hands, marvelling at the feel of his skin, warm and familiar against her own.

Many times, had she returned to him, and with each visitation, the desire to be with him had grown, until it was like a sickness within her blood, a yearning need to lay by his side. She ached to look into his eyes, to converse with him, their voices low and intimate, their gazes mingling as lovers do. Although they were not lovers, not yet.

My world, she mused. *My world is very different. Not so busy, so frantic. You people seem to never be still. Your minds are never at rest; constantly you strive and struggle for more.*

But surely, he replied, *that's how a race evolves and grows? It is that instinctive desire to survive, to improve our lives, that lifts us from mere animal status, and elevates us into higher beings. If man had not always been driven by his needs and wants, we would probably still be swinging from the trees.*

She was silent, reflecting on his words. Over time, she had become accustomed to the absence of lifesong, yet it never failed to disturb. That a whole race of people could function and survive without any sense of the great song, without being connected, still amazed, and appalled her.

The next day she had a visitor. There was no warning, no message sent in advance, instead, he merely arrived in her workshop. There was just a sudden sense of his presence; a feeling in the skin on the back of her neck that she was being observed.

She looked up, startled, her attention drawn so abruptly from the piece she was singing into creation, its lines blurred and wavered. The sharp clear image she had been striving for, melting the way ice does when touched by the first rays of the spring sun.

He stood in the doorway of her workshop; his ancient form hunched over the simple carved staff he had used since before her memories began. She leapt to her feet, her stool twisting and falling, unnoticed, behind her.

"Wise One," she cried, and bowed, clasping hands to her heart in traditional homage to the most revered ancient of the elders. A lifelong friend of her grandsire, she had never been alone with him before. Now, awash with the greatness of his lifesong, the spacious workshop seemed close and confined.

"I am honoured by your presence," she murmured when at last she dared raise her eyes to meet his – still sharp despite the greatness of his years. They twinkled benevolently at her obvious discomfort, and the crevasses of life etched deeply into his face creased further still into a gentle smile of welcome.

"Yes, yes," he waved away her stiff formality, those sharp eyes darting around the workshop at the finished pieces arranged on the shelves, and at those which were still in transit, his attention catching and narrowing at that which had been inspired by the other place, by him.

Her breath held in her chest. She knew it could not mean anything to him, yet that gaze seemed all-knowing, all-seeing as if he already knew much of what she was discovering.

"Very interesting," was all he said. "May I ask what has evoked such a radical change in style? These pieces," a wizened hand swept out, encompassing all, singling none. "I have never seen their like before."

"I … I felt it was time … for a change," she murmured, nonplussed by his question. "My grandsire's death seems to have triggered a change in direction..." her voice trailed away under the directness of his look.

"I see," he nodded once as if something of significant importance had passed between them.

"Will you do me the honour of accepting some refreshment, Wise One?" she asked, her initial shock fading enough for simple courtesy to be remembered.

She brewed tea using petals from her precious hoard of the rare and highly valued gentianna flower. This beautiful, elusive plant grew only in the highest reaches of the mountains; and she remembered the old woman who had bartered them for one of her largest and most impressive pieces.

Thankful she had saved them, she breathed deeply of its calming, exotic aroma, pouring it carefully into her most delicate cups, and arranging them pleasingly on a small, hand-painted tray. She placed spiced biscuits on a matching plate.

The smallness of the gestures helped centre her. Smoothing her countenance into one of placid enquiry, she placed the tray on the small table before him, curling herself respectfully onto a stool close by, and watched silently as he took up a cup and sniffed, eyebrows raising in surprised delight.

"Gentianna tea? This is a rare and unexpected treat, I thank you."

"You honour my dwelling, Wise One," she replied, then hesitated, wondering if she dared ask.

"What is your question, child?" he asked mildly, reaching for a spiced biscuit, crumbs scattering into the whiteness of his beard, eyes crinkling with obvious pleasure at the taste.

"I merely wonder at your presence," she replied. "I know your duties are many, and I am surprised, although, of course, deeply honoured by your visit."

"Your grandsire was my oldest and most valued friend. Is it not natural I should pay a visit to his dearly beloved grandchild? To pay my respects, and to enquire into her ... well-being?"

For a moment, her heart stilled at the knowledge she imagined she heard beneath his words. Then sense prevailed. He knew nothing, could never guess the secret which consumed her from within. Even the wisest could not imagine such a thing.

A world without lifesong was unthinkable, inconceivable, a nightmare to be awoken from with fervent relief. No, the Wise One's visit was a mere coincidence – a gesture of consideration for the grandchild of an old friend. That was all.

"I thank you for your concern, Wise One,' she replied silkily, her expression as bland as his own, "but I am well. My work keeps me much occupied."

"Ah yes, your work," he interrupted mildly, reaching for another biscuit. "Is it not a little surprising, that the passing of a grandsire should provoke such an … extreme reaction? Such a fundamental change in style and context?"

"My grandsire and I were very close," she countered, the tea hot and fragrant on her tongue. "I believe it natural his passing should have awoken a desire for change in me."

"Perhaps," the Wise One mused. He paused, sipping thoughtfully at his tea. Silence, heavy and laden with expectation, settled upon them.

Uncomfortable under the directness of his gaze, she looked down at the smallness of her feet, studying in intricate detail the curve of her toes, and the delicate carving of the rings she liked to adorn them with.

She remembered, with a sudden flush of colour to her cheeks, that the last time she had been with him, he had knelt at her feet, holding them wonderingly in his hands.

So small, he murmured. *So beautiful.*

She glanced up with a guilty start, to find the Wise One's eyes upon her, feeling the heat mount in her face. He could not know. Only her reactions would betray her. Gently, she told herself fiercely, gently...

"Child," his voice was low yet commanding, "is there something you need to tell me?"

"Wise One?" she said, just the right note of puzzled concern in her voice.

"Your grandsire," he continued, "was a good and intelligent man, wiser than you perhaps realise."

"Yes, he was," she murmured, confused by the conversational direction change.

"Were you aware, for instance, that he was invited many times to join the Council of Elders?"

Shock, painful and sharp, jolted through her. To have kept such a thing secret from her!

"I was not aware such an honour had been offered to him," she replied carefully, masking her hurt behind a facade of polite curiosity. "Tell me, Wise One, why did he refuse?"

"He had his reasons," came the obscure answer, and she frowned at a sudden thought.

"Was it because he had me to care for?" she asked slowly, and the Wise One shook his head.

"That may have been a factor," he replied. "But there were other, more pressing, demands on his time. Tell me, child, did your grandsire ever talk to you about things that possibly disturbed you?"

"Wise One?" This time she did not have to feign confusion.

"No matter," he sighed and finished his tea. Brushing crumbs from his beard he rose to go, pausing in the doorway to study her, his expression gravely serious. "If you ever feel troubled by anything or require my assistance in any way... send for me, and I will come, day or night."

"I thank you, Wise One,' she said. 'But I do not see..."

"Anything," he repeated, fixing her with a gaze of such intensity, that she felt her soul revealed before it. "Your grandsire was a very special man, as were your parents. You are their child. I feel an obligation to protect you."

"Protect me, Wise One? Protect me from what?"

"Remember," he said, and was gone, leaving her uncomfortably wondering at the strangeness of the encounter, aware for the first time of secrets from the past. Secrets involving her grandsire and, possibly, her parents?

She shook her head in confusion, longing for nightfall when it would be safe to securely close the door to her dwelling and travel to that other place. To him – and to a world which was rapidly becoming more real, and more important, than her own.

Chapter Five
The Joining

When night finally wrapped its velvet mantle around the world, she fled to him, impatient to touch, to feel. More unsettled by the visit of the Wise One than she cared to admit, she felt an urgency grip her. When she opened her eyes and he was before her, she reached for him, hungry with need.

His eyes widened yet he spoke not, merely letting her take him where she would, slowing only when he realised it was her first time, holding back and gently soothing where she would have rushed.

Quickly her body learnt this new, its rhythm pounding through her blood, singing through her heart and soul, their voices rising together in blissful harmony.

Later, they lay quietly, their bodies entwined and instinctively she reached for him with her lifesong. She found only emptiness – the smallness of his soul trapped within a single body.

Disappointed, she sang to him, the wonder of the act of love empowering her song until it swelled and burst from its confines.

She heard him gasp and realised he could not accept such a joining. It was too much. It would burn him out from within, yet it would not be contained. For the first time, she ventured forth from his presence and the containment of his dwelling.

Onwards and upwards she journeyed, seeing his world spread out in its entirety below her.

She danced and spiralled, flashing through clouds so fast she felt only the briefest touch of moisture on her cheek. She laughed aloud at such exhilaration. The sun was warm on her face.

The beauty of his world filled her with pleasure. Reaching out with her lifesong she sought connections and found many. Hundreds, thousands, millions, billions. This world teemed with lifesong, as its creatures busied themselves with their lives.

She free fell, honing in on the songs, picking out individual beings to share, for the briefest of moments, their existence and lifesong...

A great black and white seagoing mammal – it leapt from the surface of a rolling mighty ocean, its lifesong exulting its joy to be alive. For a second, she shared consciousness. In that second, she lived its whole life, felt the rush of salt water past its flanks, the thrill of twisting through the swell of the waves...

An ant – much like those on her world, scurrying briskly to its nest. Its industriousness humbled her, the intensity of its need to care for its colony and its queen...

A coiled, basking snake – the sun warming its chilly blood, the scent of prey tasted in the air...

A small, rodent-like creature – nimbly climbing behind the walls of a dwelling, whiskers twitching, fear pounding its heart, the desire for food driving it forwards...

A great, lumbering grey beast – baggy skin creasing under a hot, unrelenting sun, the relief of wet mud, the tightly knit family community without which it could not survive...

A shining, leaping fish – desperately battling its way upstream, the urgent, survivalist need to procreate forcing it ever upwards...

A bird – its wings glossy black, gliding on a thermal, surveying, hunting, the excited jerk of its body at the spotting of the smaller bird far below...

Another great sea mammal – this one large and ponderous, its lifesong an audible thing of beauty, booming out across the waves...

She lived them all. In that single moment she lived all the lifesongs of the world, and it was glorious. For a second. Then, death and disaster crowded in.

Natural death was to be expected; it did not taint the great song; it was within the order of things. But this ... this deliberate poisoning of the rivers and the seas ... she gasped and choked with those that depended on the purity of its waters…

The annihilation of the mighty forests, the lungs of this world. The planet struggled to breathe, and she struggled with it, feeling the incomprehension and fear of the forest dwellers fleeing before the obliteration of their homes, the great crying out of the trees which fell before their time…

The over-farming of the land, the stripping away of its goodness and the choking of its natural defences with polluting chemicals…

The fouling of the very air itself until creatures struggled for breath.

In particular – a striped, winged insect battled to cope with the changes wrought in its world. As she briefly shared its lifesong, she realised the importance of this creature. That, should it be exterminated, the plants on this world would not be pollinated and would die – along with every other creature.

All were so interlinked in a beautiful and elegant ecosystem of co-dependence, that removing one tiny, seemingly insignificant player, could result in extinction for all...

Everywhere she looked was death and senseless destruction – a world being destroyed, raped, stripped of its assets. A world hellbent on ecological suicide...

Angrily, she searched for the culprit and did not have far to look – his race, his species. Hot urgent greed, the ambition she sensed within him. She saw it now, forced to the bitter conclusion, saw the sweetness of the world trampled underfoot without heed or thought by a desperate need for more and more.

Screaming with horror, she recoiled from the image, retreating into herself, opening her eyes to find herself staring into his concerned blue gaze.

Where did you go? he demanded, worry sharpening his tone. *Your body stayed here, but you ... where did you go?*

Your world, she gasped, her heart still pounding with the enormity of what she had seen.

Your world is so beautiful and yet ... you are killing it, taking, and taking with no thought for tomorrow. Everything is dying. You are destroying it all, and soon there will be nothing left. Nothing!

Nothing left? he frowned. *No, surely, it's not that bad? I know there are issues ... the rainforests, some animals are close to extinction.*

You are all close to extinction! she cried. *It is almost too late. You have almost reached the point where it will be impossible to turn back, to save what is left! Oh, so much death and destruction! You are a planet of fools. You have but one world and you are busy destroying it. Don't you care? Can't you see what you are doing?*

Yes, but ... he paused, plainly confused, and agitated at the direction she had taken so soon after the sublime joining of their bodies.

But what can be done? he demanded. *Tell me, what can be done to stop this? To save our planet.*

You must cease this brutal pillaging of your world's resources. Your planet is so rich. It could supply all you needed, were it managed, correctly harvested, and respected. If you were to work with nature, instead of merely taking with no thought or heed for those who are to come after you.

But I am just one man, he insisted, his tone bitter with weary resignation. *What can I do, alone?*

It is true, you are just one voice, but surely there must be others? She pressed her hands to her heart and felt its frantic pulsing at the intensity of her need to convince him. *Perhaps all it will take is for one man to say stop, enough, for others to then have the courage to also speak out.*

Perhaps. He did not sound convinced, and she saw from his face she had failed to impress upon him the true scale of what she had seen, what she had felt.

He reached for her. Willingly she submitted, desperate to find oblivion in his body; to forget, if only for a while, the images still fresh in her mind.

Later, when the echoes of their cries of release had long faded from the room and he lay silently sleeping; she slipped quietly away to her world...

Chapter Six
The World

She did not return to him for many days, needing the peace and tranquillity of her world to restore and replenish her lifesong, which she felt had been depleted and tarnished by its contact with the all-encompassing greed of his world.

She rested, sleeping dreamlessly every night, moving through the days slowly and deliberately. Not working, not seeing another living soul, enjoying protracted moments of stillness when the vast rolling cadences of the great song lapped at her consciousness. Finally, she felt strong enough to return to him, drawn by the needs and wants of her newly awakened body. Craving him ... his touch, his voice, his look. Yearning to feel again his body moving joyously within hers, she could not stay away another moment.

In the unblinking of an eye, she was beside him, catching him on the cusp of wakefulness. He blinked in incomprehension, as she hungrily took from him that which she so ardently needed. Within moments, his urgency matched her own, and they plundered each other's bodies, riding the crest of splintering desire.

Their hands, mouths, and hearts, locked in a dance as old as time, until they fell apart, sated, and drained, their breathing harsh and ragged in the still, predawn hush of his room.

Once again, her lifesong soared free of the confines of her body. Curious about his world and its people, she deliberately sought them out, probing and examining. She wished to learn, to understand, how a race of people with no concept of lifesong could exist, and how an entire planet could have seemingly agreed on such a mutually destructive path.

An elderly woman lay in a small room, ripe with her squalid presence. She felt the woman's fear, shocked that a revered and wise elder should be reduced to such an existence.

At the very last gasp of life, she sensed the woman's dread of dying alone, of passing into nothingness, a life wasted and empty, offspring that wounded with unthinking lack of care.

Heart brimming with sympathy, she gathered her lifesong and sang into the woman, soothing, easing her transition over the threshold. The woman gave a great, shuddering breath. She felt her slip peacefully away, a blissfully happy smile lighting up her wrinkled face, a smile which would ease a guilty family when her body was discovered days later.

Angrily, she soared away, comparing this woman's miserable end with the respect the elderly on her world were afforded. Valued for their knowledge, for the richness of their lifesong, she knew the people of her world would be shocked at the idea of an elder dying alone, without their family and friends all around them, and she bitterly wondered.

What kind of a world was this that could treat its elders so?

A girl, little more than a child, covered her eyes with her hands as if this would be enough to hide her from his vicious intentions. Still, he found her, his violence brutal and shocking. She cried in horror, but fists were merely the beginning. Disbelievingly, she suffered with the child as her young, tender body was invaded, flesh bruising under the onslaught, sobs and cries for mercy falling on deaf ears.

Powerless to prevent the atrocity she was watching, she moved through the child's mind, smothering it under a blanket of blessed unconsciousness. She filled the darkness with images of her world, placing a tiny piece of her lifesong into the child's soul, so the truth of beauty and love would remain with the child for the whole of her miserable, mercifully short, existence. She knew when the child awoke the horror of her life would still be there, yet at least she had provided the child with a bolt hole, a refuge to escape to in times of extreme need.

She moved on, unable to bear it any longer, into the mind of another child. A boy this time, his body gaunt and stunted through the effects of lifelong, severe malnutrition. Barefoot and ragged, his hunger burnt as a constant, ignored fact, and around him, she felt others like him.

Realisation dawned that in the absence of actual family, this disenfranchised little band of tattered urchins had come together in a mutual joining of support and need. One that offered a rough and ready kind of love and stability.

She felt their fear and struggled to comprehend that this group of mere children were also somehow prey. She saw men, identical in attire, track and follow the children. Not understanding, she watched as they pointed shiny sticks at them. There was a dreadful noise, and the children scattered, yet two did not rise. She saw the emptiness in their still young yet painfully old eyes, the spreading puddle of red beneath them, and knew they would never run with the pack again. And then she perceived the shiny sticks were terrible weapons of some kind, weapons to rip apart the childish flesh of the innocent. Horrified, she moved on.

What kind of a world was this that could treat its children so?

She found a building, large and imposing, bustling with unceasing activity. Curious, she swept through it, recoiling at the tide of sickness and misery which engulfed her, realising this to be a healing centre of sorts.

She saw the efforts of the healers to cope with the huge diversity and range of illnesses. Diseases of the mind and of the body, a few of which she recognised and could have healed herself in an instant, was she on her world with access to her stock of powerful herbs and healing roots. Many of the diseases, however, were shocking and alien; terrible disharmonies within bodies deprived of the natural restorative properties of their lifesong. Bodies that had turned on themselves, poisoning and contaminating their precious organs, consuming them from within.

Comprehension dawned that without lifesong this world had turned to increasingly artificial and intrusive methods with which to heal their sick, causing new, more virulent diseases to be created. In turn, this meant that ever more extreme treatments had to be used, and so on and so on, creating a downward spiral of cause and effect. The healers were, on the whole, good people, committed to helping, but there were simply too many to cope with. She saw weary resignation amongst them, and the unspoken acknowledgement that they were merely fire-fighting – delaying the inevitable.

She saw much that sickened and bewildered her. People alone, afraid and in pain, left to call for help, unanswered and unaided by healers too sick at heart themselves to come to their assistance. Hurriedly, she left.

What kind of a world was this that could treat its sick so?

A baby, innocent and newborn. She peered wonderingly at its blank mind, rich with potential and possibilities, yet still, the stain which tainted the rest of the world lurked within its soul. The complete absence of lifesong seemed even more shocking than in the adults.

She remembered the few times she had been present at the birth of new life on her world, when the great song had rolled and gloried all around, heralding the triumphant renewal of life.

How different here. From the moment of birth until the last gasp of death, the people of this world struggled in a futile and pointless battle against themselves. Always at war, always at want. Greed and petty spite ate away at their souls until nothing mattered. She saw from the earliest point of life, children encouraged to strive and want, to take and dominate.

What kind of a world was this that could treat itself so?

Abruptly, bone-weary, and soul-sick of all she had seen and experienced, she wished herself home, startled when she struggled to return. Accustomed to a smooth, almost imperceptible transition between worlds, this sensation of wading through clinging, dragging matter alarmed her, almost as if the contamination of his world had infected her and was dragging her down to its level, and she was greatly relieved when she finally opened her eyes to find her own tranquil and peaceful dwelling once more cradling her in its arms.

Chapter Seven
The Loss

For many days after, it seemed she had carried back some of the despair and hopelessness of his world. Weary and chilled to the bone, she stayed within the refuge of her dwelling, huddled by the fire, eating little, fortifying herself with healing tinctures, and wrinkling her nose at their bitter taste.

Her lifesong seemed weak, insubstantial as if his world had drained some of her precious essences. Alarmed, she did not allow herself to travel back to him, giving herself time to consider all she had experienced, all she had learnt, allowing herself time to heal.

Great was her relief when, as the days slipped by, she felt her energy returning until her lifesong rolled and swelled within her as strongly as before.

He called to her. Every night, as she lay wide-eyed and restless in her narrow, lonely bed, she felt him calling. His need and desire were a tangible rushing force, compelling itself across the void which separated them, tugging, and insisting. At last, hungry for him, she overcame her fear and returned.

They did not speak; words were unnecessary. Hands and mouths sought and found each other, bodies connected and re-connected. Again, and again, she cried out in shocked and awed wonder at the gift of pleasure he gave.

Her body arched off the bed, taut as a bow, before collapsing into boneless gasping ecstasy, clutching him to her, his breathing hoarse and ragged on her neck. Hearts beat fiercely against each other, as she realised in that moment how much she loved him, and how difficult it would be to leave him again.

For days she stayed with him, unthinking and uncaring of the shell of her body she had left behind in her world.

Fuelled by a mutual hunger, they existed in a kind of limbo, separate from either of their worlds, a time apart, where the only reality was each other and the urgent desire they had to touch, to hold, to love. To simply be.

And when he slept, her soul soared upwards and away – morbid fascination forcing her to explore his world once again.

She saw families struggling to survive – parents descending to any level to obtain food for their starving children...

She saw perpetual warfare – whole races of people singled out to be slaughtered and discriminated against, the legacy of fear, intolerance and hatred being passed down through the generations.

She saw children – so young their bones had barely had time to form – forced to take up weapons and fight...

She saw individuals – trapped in pointless, joyless existence, condemned to a treadmill of nagging, petty discontent, until at last it curdled their souls and they crept noiselessly to their graves, leaving behind an uncaring world which did not even notice their passing. Wasted lives; wasted opportunities.

She watched in helpless disbelieving horror as half the world starved, whilst the other half gorged in a self-destruction of gluttony, their abused bodies bloated and miserable, their flesh groaning in desolation and self-loathing.

And everywhere – overlaying every scrap of existence – was violence and the fear of violence.

Night after night she travelled the world – forcing herself to look, to witness the atrocities the people of his planet visited upon each other and upon themselves.

Night after night as she moved amongst them, she tried to touch as many unhappy souls with her lifesong as she could. Aware that she could barely scratch the surface of the suffering, still she tried. Soothing damaged minds, comforting injured hearts, she looked for the neediest; the most desperate to aid, but the task was too vast. For the first time in her life, she felt the chill grip of despair.

And every morning she returned to him, exhausted and sick to her very heart, the blank desolation in her eyes conveying to him a taste of the horrors she had witnessed.

Scared for her, he pleaded with her to remain safe by his side. But every night he would wake and realise she was not there, that only the shell of her being remained, cold and lifeless.

He would wait and watch, fretful and anxious, until colour would return to her waxen cheeks and her beautiful eyes would open and stare at him, shocked and unblinking. Her gaze accusing, condemning. He noticed how her peaceful contentment dimmed a little more with each passing day, how her flesh grew pale, and her eyes dulled.

Worried, he begged her to stop, but she could not, her nocturnal wanderings as addictive as any drug, her need to try to heal these people becoming more urgent.

It was before dawn. Silently, she slipped into her body and opened her eyes. The room, his room, was dim, and she blinked several times before scattered senses could comprehend what she was seeing.

His back was to her, fingers moving in ceaseless energy over what she had been told was called a laptop. Unable to understand how he filled his days, she only knew he mostly worked from home, as she did, yet there any similarities between them ended.

He did not seem to create anything, either practical or beautiful. Concerned, she had asked him how he lived. With nothing to offer in trade, how did he eat, clothe himself and furnish his dwelling?

His brow had furrowed, before clearing in relieved understanding.

Your society exists on a bartering system?

Yes, does not yours?

No, oh no, well, perhaps amongst primitive people.

Primitive?

I mean less socially advanced.

He paused, seeing from her expression that she was offended, and he hurriedly continued.

No, we work in exchange for money, and then we use this money to buy what we need.

At first, the concept was confusing, then, with time, she had come to understand that this system explained so much that was wrong with his world. Why some seemed to have so much, and some seemed to have so little.

She had tried, haltingly, to clarify her feelings to him.

On my world, everyone has a talent, a skill. From childhood, their lifesong guides them towards this calling, be it making something practical, like clothing, or a necessary skill such as healing. Perhaps a person has a talent for creating things of beauty, things people admire and with which they want to adorn themselves and their homes. I am a sculptor. My lifesong enables me to see beneath the surface of a piece of wood or stone and sing forth its true shape. People like what I have created and offer in exchange their produce or skills.

He had been silent for a moment, thinking about what she had said. *What about if someone has no talent for anything?* he finally asked.

Everyone has a skill, even if it is merely for tending the earth. On my world, that is as valued as the most talented of healers. Everyone is necessary to maintain society and has a vital role to play. On your world, there seem to be so many with no place ... so many angry, frustrated disconnected beings. They feel society does not need them, so, in turn, they absolve themselves from the rules that bind a strong society together, becoming like monsters, hurting so much inside they must lash out at others in turn.

That's true enough, he replied ruefully.

Now she lay quietly on the bed, attempting to re-connect with her lifesong, feeling the rawness inside where pieces of herself had been torn out in increasingly smaller portions to aid the poor, wretched souls she discovered on her nightly travels.

Unaware of her return, he worked on.

Wearied beyond belief, she did not speak, did not let him know she had returned. Instead, her eyes wandered the now-familiar room, finally alighting on the flickering screen on the wall.

She knew its name, knew it to be a device that showed a confusing array of facts and stories. He had even attempted to explain to her how it worked, yet her mind had been unable to grasp the concept. In the end, she simply had to accept it was yet another example of how different their two worlds were.

The sound was muted. Sleepily, she watched as some vast, gleaming white piece of machinery forged upwards into a blue sky, and then an image was shown of a world, silent and beautiful, its blue seas wreathed in drifts of white. Shocked, she pulled herself upwards on the bed.

He turned at the sound, his expression registering relief at her return.

What is that? she asked, pointing at the screen.

Puzzled, he followed the direction of the gesture.

It's the Earth, he replied simply.

What is the earth?

What is the ...? Well, it's my world, this planet.

But how are you seeing it? Without your lifesong to take you to the stars, without that connection to the great song, how is it possible for you to view your world?

We don't need a lifesong or whatever. There was a hint of arrogance in his tone. *Man has been to the moon, there are satellites in space, the space shuttle goes into orbit regularly, and there was even a space station up there.*

Satellites ... shuttle? Her words floundered in confusion. Patiently, quietly, he explained it all to her, until finally she understood and shrank back onto the bed in horror.

You seek to travel the stars without knowing the first thing about them?

We understand them, he retorted, stung by the incredulous tone of her voice.

No, she shook her head adamantly. *You know nothing about them, how can you? Without the great song you are merely children, attempting to walk alone in the darkness, unsuspecting of what lies out there, or the harm you may do to others. Perhaps unintentionally, it is true, nonetheless, your race will blunder into the delicate structure of the universe, carrying your contagion with you.*

That's a bit much, he protested hotly. *You talk as if we're some kind of evil beings, monsters.*

You are, she replied flatly. *Oh, I know most of you do not mean to be, most of your race do not intend harm, yet still, harm others you must. It is the way your species has survived – at the expense of others. It is programmed into you, even within your babies. The need to satisfy the self is the most overwhelming urge they possess.*

Exhausted, she lay still and closed her eyes, feeling his wounded silence in the room. She was unable to speak anymore... to tell him of the beauty and majesty that lay out there, its intricate subtlety which could be so easily damaged or even destroyed.

Finally, he sighed, a heavy exhalation of concern, and moved to sit beside her on the bed. She felt it dip under his weight, yet extreme lethargy gripped her and still, she did not move.

Are you all right?

She sensed the moment his annoyance changed to concern. Touched, she attempted to reach out to him with her lifesong, to caress, to reassure him.

It was not there.

Her eyes flew open meeting his mildly worried gaze with a panic-stricken stare of her own.

What is it? What's the matter?

His voice was taut with anxiety, and she gagged on the lump of terror forming in her throat.

It's gone!

What is? What's gone?

My lifesong, it's gone, I can no longer feel it!

It'll come back, he reassured. *You know how weak you are when you return.*

No, this is different! she insisted. *Always before my lifesong was weak, yes, but still it was there. Now it's gone, I can no longer feel it, I'm no longer connected to the great song!*

Stinging tears welled in her eyes. Desperately she sought – deeper and deeper – probing violently for that which had been lost.

Attempting to console her, he pulled her into his arms. She fought him, clawing at her face and hair in soul-ripping despair.

I feel nothing! she screamed. *I am nothing! How can you people live like this? So alone! So very, very alone!*

Sobbing, she finally allowed him to hold her, clinging to his body, her despair engulfing them both.

Later, the violence of the emotional storm abated, and she lay quietly beside him. Numb with the horror of her loss, his words – meant to reassure and soothe – washed over her as if they were nothing.

Sleep, he urged her. *Rest. Perhaps that's what your body needs. Sleep now, and when you wake up, it'll be back. Your lifesong will be back as strong as ever.*

She did not believe him, yet wanted to, clutching desperately at the hope. Closing her eyes, she felt the black pull of exhausted slumber, allowing herself to tip over the edge into it.

Days drifted, and so did she. Time had no meaning, she simply existed. She felt his concern and fear. It could not touch her.

Softly, she was aware of all that she was, all she had been, and all she could have become, melting away like a snow sculpture left too long in the sun, her body liquefying, her features blurring.

Without lifesong there was no meaning, no cohesion to hold her together and so she began to let go.

On the fourth day, his control snapped. Striding to the bed, he gathered her up in his arms and shook her, his expression contorted with angry distress.

You can't go on like this. You must go home. Perhaps there you can heal yourself.

I don't want to leave you. She dragged her scattered wits together to answer.

And I don't want you to go, he stressed. *But neither can I sit here and just watch while you fade away. I can't let you die, not when there may be some way to save you.*

Going home may not save me, she murmured, and he released her back onto the bed, running trembling hands through his hair.

Maybe not, he agreed. *But if you stay here you will die. At least if you go back, there is a chance that your people could help you. Perhaps this Wise One you spoke of.*

Perhaps, she echoed softly.

An image of the Wise One's face, concerned and knowing, crept across her eyes. The thought occurred again – how much had he known? Looking back, it seemed he had been warning her as if he somehow realised what she was experiencing.

You must go back, he said again. She looked at him, saw the worry etched deeply into his features, and realised what it would mean to him if she were to die.

Another loss, just like before. She had thought love would be enough to keep her here, but now understood she had been wrong.

All right, she whispered, feeling the sting of hot tears inside her eyes. *But I will miss you.*

I will miss you too, he replied, his gaze steady and warming on her pale face.

But at least I'll know you're alive somewhere in the universe, and maybe one day you'll be able to come back.

Maybe, she agreed, but as she spoke the words, she understood them to be a lie.

Go now, he urged. *Go before you become so weak you can't.*

I love you.

She gave him the words as a parting gift, saw the smile slip onto his lips as she closed her eyes, and felt for the link.

I love you too.

She heard him as she reached out with everything she had, seeking that strong silver thread that always pulled her home. Over and again, she probed, searching, grasping, fumbling for it, but it was like trying to find a needle in a dark room.

In despair, she opened her eyes once again to his concerned face.

Go, he urged. *You must go.*

I cannot, she sobbed. *The connection is broken, I can never go home again!*

Chapter Eight
The Teacher

Cold, she was so cold. Huddled beneath piles of covers, her body now barely enough of a presence to raise them more than a few inches, she moved in and out of a fugue state. In her more lucid moments, she wondered what was happening to the outer husk of the body she had left behind on her world. Was it dying too, withering away like an un-watered plant?

Vaguely, she was aware of him moving about the room. Often, he came to her side. Once she heard him sobbing and pacing, railing at some god. She wanted to comfort, to assure him it was not his fault, that she had chosen this path, but the effort to move was too much. Gratefully, she let the darkness close over her once again.

Suddenly, she was jerked from her state of lethargy as he threw back the covers and lifted her, gently thrusting her arms into the sleeves of a large, woollen garment, slipping thick socks onto her feet. Feebly, she protested, her hands fluttering to his arms like a bird's wings beating on a windowpane.

Come on, he said. *Please try to help me. We must go out and it's so cold, you'll need to be well wrapped up to keep you warm.*

No, she murmured. *Where? Leave me alone and let me die in peace.*

I couldn't just sit here doing nothing, he stated flatly. S*o, I googled lifesong. I didn't expect to find anything relevant, but I did, I did.*

His words were strange and meaningless to her. Numbly, she stared at him.

There's a place, he continued. *A sort of retreat, almost what you'd call a monastery, only not religious. Well, not a recognised religion. It doesn't have a website, and from what I can gather they shun all modern technology, but the founder once gave an interview. That's what Google took me to*

– the interview. In it, he says the retreat aims to attempt to reconnect people to their lifesong.

He cannot mean lifesong in the true sense, she whispered, her mind dazed by his words. *He cannot, it must be a coincidence.*

Probably, he agreed, wrapping a thick, well-lined coat around her wraith-like form, *but it's worth a try. Anything is better than just sitting here, watching you …*

He stopped and swallowed hard, busying himself with placing a warm scarf about her neck, and a hat on her head. In her mind, she completed his sentence – anything was better than sitting there watching her die.

She realised in an instant she must allow him to do this, that his very nature would not tolerate inactivity. In all her nocturnal travelling around his world, she had come to understand his species a little and knew passive acceptance was not a prevalent trait.

There's no email, no phone, he continued briskly, leading her towards the door. *But there's an address and it's not far away – about thirty miles. If we go now, we'll miss the traffic.*

Very well, she murmured, leaning against him, her strength almost completely gone.

Outside the door to his home stretched a long, dimly lit corridor. Unable to deal with any more unfamiliar stimuli, she merely closed her senses to it all, turning her face into his shoulder, as he led her into a small, box-like room, lined with mirrors. For the first time, she saw herself as she appeared to him – so thin, so insubstantial – her huge topaz eyes the only alive part of her features. The floor lurched and she uttered a breathy cry, clutching at him for support, feeling their rapid descent with terror. Softly, he reassured, holding her steady, lending his strength.

When the box room finally stopped, an eternity later, she was relieved when the door silently slid open to reveal a dark subterranean world filled with fantastical objects. Numb with incomprehension, she watched in silence as he lifted his arm and pressed a small item clasped between his fingers, catching her breath when one of the curious objects abruptly flashed lights at them and uttered a strange clicking noise.

He took her to it, opening a part of it to reveal comfortable, well-padded seats inside, and she slid gratefully down into the object, feeling the give of leather beneath her. Gently, he fastened some sort of strap across her chest and lap, before closing the door. Hurrying round to the other side of the object, he clambered into another seat, identical to her own, yet placed behind some sort of wheel.

The small device with which he had awoken the object, he now fitted into a hole located under the wheel, turned it and the object burst into throaty angry life. Unable to control herself, she moaned with fear and grabbed the edge of the seat, turning large, terrified eyes upon him.

What is this thing? she gasped, her heart thudding with anxiety as the object moved.

It's called a car, he replied.

A car? But how...?

Look, he interrupted, his manner almost brisk, and she sensed his relief that finally, he was doing something. *Do you have carts or wagons on your world?*

Carts? Yes, of course.

Well, this is a kind of mechanised cart.

Oh, I see.

And she did see, understanding his race would never be satisfied with the simple yet infinitely practical cart. They would always strive to make it quicker, faster, and better until eventually, they arrived at machinery which could explore the stars.

Stars. As they left the underground cavern and emerged into the crystalline beauty of a wintry night, she tipped her head back and saw, through the curiously pointless window above her head, the dazzling canopy of stars spread out across the inky black sky. Different from the constellations viewed from her world, and without the connection to them her lifesong would have afforded, looking at them was like catching glimpses of freedom through the bars of a prison, tantalising, but unreachable.

It's about an hour's drive, he stated, handling the car skilfully, moving to avoid the other cars that, even at this late hour, thronged all around them. *Why don't you try and get some sleep?*

Nodding wearily, she rested her head back against the comfort of the padded leather seat, feeling her eyelids droop and sleep claim her.

A thin grey dawn had broken when she awoke, neck stiff from too long in one position, mind clouded from a deep, dreamless sleep. For moments she merely blinked, becoming aware the car had stopped moving and he was gone.

Panic had her pulling herself upright, searching for him, and finding him standing before a large pair of imposing solid-looking wooden gates. His back to her, he appeared to be arguing with a solemn-faced young man who peered at him through a small hatchway set in the impenetrable mass of wood.

Wishing to be with him, her hands beat uselessly at the door. Unable to discover how it opened, by chance, she pressed a button, the glass windowpane slid down, and their words floated to her on the still, early morning air.

You must help us, please … she's dying!

Well, take her to a hospital. This is a closed order, no visitors.

Please, we've come so far.

I'm sorry, there's nothing we can do to help.

She heard the steel in the young man's voice and knew it to be over. Their last hope, if indeed it had ever been a hope, had come to nothing.

In despair, she leant back and closed her eyes, reaching out with every fibre of her being in one last attempt at a connection to anyone, anything. She did not want to die all alone, so far away from home. A spark of life flickered within her – small and inconsequential – still, it was the best she could manage. She flung it from her, out into the world, hoping against hope some creature would take pity on her, would offer a scrap of comfort in her last, desperate moments of life.

A mere chord, it was only the briefest of resonance. But for a second it seemed to her she felt an answering echo. Faint, so faint though, as if far away something had heard and understood, had maybe even sent a soft reply. It was too little, too late, and with a sigh, her head fell forward.

Dimly, she felt the car door being wrenched open, his arms around her, undoing the strap which bound her and holding her close to his chest, his sobs echoing in her ear, his breath warm on her neck.

Please, he moaned. *Don't go, don't leave me! Wait.*

Her eyes fluttered half-open; it was the young man from the gate. Wearing an expression of intense and puzzling disapproval, he strode towards the car. She frowned slightly. His clothes, what was it about his clothes? For some reason, they reminded her of home.

You must come with me, the young man ordered. *He wants to see you.*

Too weak to stand now, she was carried hastily inside the enclosure, where she was dimly aware of silent echoing corridors, of a room so still and peaceful, and a figure waiting. Waiting for her.

He turned at their approach, his hand reaching for her, his touch on her brow soothing. Then she felt it…

… a whisper of lifesong. It trickled into her. A tiny stream of essential, life-renewing energy and she gulped at it like a person dying of thirst at the first taste of water.

But that's impossible … she murmured, and the stranger smiled.

Oh, child; you poor, lost child…

The room in which she awoke was very pleasing. Simply furnished, it reminded her of home, and this comforted her. She stirred in the narrow bed, and he turned away from the window at the sound, relief leaping into his eyes. She wondered how long he had stood there, and how long she had slept.

Where am I? What happened? she asked, probing her mind for memories.

You slept for so long, he replied, his face crinkling with love as he moved to sit beside her on the bed, helping her to sit.

We're in the retreat still, the teacher, he … well, I'm not sure what he did. He touched your head and it pulled you back. You were so close to death. I could see it on your face.

The teacher? she murmured enquiringly.

Yes, that's what he's known as apparently, he pulled a rueful face. *Frankly, he can call himself whatever he pleases, I'm just relieved he could help.*

She nodded slowly, remembering the incredible, impossible feel of his lifesong; faint, barely there, yet it had been enough to stop her slipping away, enough to hold her here, for now.

He wants to see you, he continued. *When you're ready, he wants to see you again.*

The same steely-eyed young man led them again to the room she had only the vaguest memories of. Its aura was one of peace and warmth, and she felt the sunlight as it streamed through the windows, stirring her chilly blood. Blinking at the dust motes which danced in the columns of light, they slowly paced towards the still, expectant figure that awaited them.

A handsbreadth away she stopped. He was a stranger to her, yet something called. Something nagged at her to remember.

Do I ... do I know you? she asked, her voice a whisper, and he smiled, his expression wistful almost sorrowful.

Once, perhaps, he murmured. His hand rested on her brow, and she felt it again, that flicker of a lifesong, tantalising and elusive.

On her world, the possessor of such a weak lifesong would be considered close to death, or a creature of the lowest denomination, but here, on this barren and soulless planet, it was as welcome as an oasis would be in the middle of a heat-scorched desert.

But there was something else … something in the very nature of the lifesong itself. Something long forgotten; something familiar.

How is this possible? Here, on this world, where the creatures of the sea, sky, and land all have lifesongs and yet none of its people do. I thought myself alone…

And yet, here I am, he mused. Then, reaching his hands to his face, he passed them over his eyes, doing something she did not understand. His hands fell to his side, and she stared with disbelief into his topaz gaze.

Father?

Chapter Nine
The Reunion

I do not understand. How is it you are here?
They sat before a fire, its glowing heart casting living shadows of heat over their faces. Wonderingly, she turned to look at her father, her hand still clasped tightly in his, the expression in his eyes warming her every bit as much as the fire.

What did your grandsire tell you?

Nothing, that is nothing that would explain your presence here. He told me you had died at sea, along with my mother...

She let the name linger in the air between them, needing an answer, yet reluctant to ask outright. He sighed, the affection in his eyes for her dimming into sorrow for the loss of his love.

Your mother died shortly after we were stranded here. She was simply not strong enough to survive without her lifesong.

As I was not?

As you were not, he agreed. *Maybe it is inherent in females; that need for connection, the despair of loneliness. It is something which still requires a great deal of study. Perhaps if I …*

Please, she begged, dragging his attention back. *Please tell me how you came to be here, how I came to be here. What happened to us?*

It has long been known that our family is… different from others, he began. *Our lifesong is powerful, and yet, it is not only that. It seems to enable us to travel further than any other, to seek out mysteries. That desire to explore, to know, to understand, is an overwhelming trait of our bloodline.*

Yes, she murmured in agreement, reflecting on her life, the constant questioning of her grandsire, her need to understand all around her, and their heated debates on life on other worlds. Never had she repeated these discussions to another living soul.

Only now did she question her motives for keeping it secret. Was it because she had known, instinctively, that none besides themselves would have understood?

Your grandsire, my father, had dabbled with such explorations, projecting his mind further and further; attempting to contact lives on other worlds. His efforts though, all seemed doomed to failure, until we – for by that time I was working alongside him –discovered it was possible to project not just your mind, but your essence as well. That the body could be split into four components – not three as had previously been believed – your soul, your mind, and of course, your physical outer shell. But there was a fourth, inner layer, like a membrane; a skin beneath the skin, which could also be projected, along with your soul and your mind, leaving just the outer husk, the shell of your physical body behind.

Like an onion, her lover, silent until now, murmured behind them, and her father turned pleased eyes upon him.

Yes, that is an entirely accurate analogy. We discovered our body was made of these layers which could be separated, like an onion, and our family, alone amongst our species, had this ability.

So, this fourth layer, this membrane, this is what I am now? she asked, touching her cold skin disbelievingly, seeing for herself how insubstantial, how translucent, it appeared.

Yes, it promotes just enough physical presence to allow you to feel and touch, and to be touched in return, he concluded, mouth twisting in a wry grin as he glanced over at her lover. She felt a momentary flush of discomfort, knowing he had accurately guessed the relationship between them.

So, you travelled to this world?

Yes.

With my mother?

Yes.

But how was that possible? You said only those of our bloodline had the ability?

That is correct, but your mother was the child of your grandsire's sister, so she shared the same bloodline. All the same, she did not possess the ability I did. She could travel, but only if I accompanied her, and she lacked the strength to attempt the task herself.

What happened to her? she asked slowly, needing to know, yet at the same time, afraid to hear.

Something went wrong, he met her gaze with regretful eyes. *I miscalculated and we stayed too long, the malaise on this world infected us and dissolved the link. By the time I realised what was happening, it was too late. I tried to send your mother back alone, but it was no use. The thread which tied us to our physical bodies was gone, and we were too weak, our lifesongs too drained, to even attempt the journey unaided.*

For long moments he remained silent, his stare hooded and turned towards the flames as if remembering things buried deep … things that pained to be recalled.

For weeks we remained in hiding, resting, and praying that our lifesongs would recover. They never did. Gradually, your mother grew weaker, until she simply faded away and was gone. For days I clung to the hope that perhaps the dissolution of her presence on this world was enough to somehow catapult her back into her body on our world. But, had that happened, I knew my father would have found some way to reach me. Perhaps he could not have managed it alone, but with the combined lifesongs of the Council of Elders, he would have been able to …

The Council of Elders? she interrupted him, startled. *Did they know what you were doing?*

Of course, he replied, surprised. *We would never have attempted such a thing without their permission and guidance. Indeed, were it not for their generosity in providing for us, so we did not have to be concerned with our everyday needs, it would have been more difficult for us to find the time.*

Funding the space project … her lover murmured, and her father started slightly in his seat, then looked thoughtful, nodding his head as if in sudden realisation.

How did you survive? she asked, reaching to take his other hand in her own, feeling the warmth of his touch in stark contrast to the coldness of her own.

I do not know, he replied slowly. *Perhaps, being male, I was naturally stronger than your mother. I only know that I did survive, and gradually, I began to make a life for myself on this poor, benighted world. My lifesong did not return, and the tiny scrap I had remaining I hoarded jealously, understanding that should it ever completely deplete, I too would simply dissipate into nothing.*

But you gave some to me, she cried, horrified at what this might mean.

The tiniest whisper, he dismissed her worries with an airy wave. *Do not fear, I have enough still.*

She nodded, still concerned, then looked around the room, aware of the strangeness of the place she had found him in, remembering the young man who had admitted them.

Father, what is this place? What have you become?

I am the Teacher, he proclaimed, a little pompously she thought. *I guide and teach others and help them to re-connect with their lifesong. I attempt to awaken long-dormant memories and skills in these people, so that they may once again take their places within the great song.*

Is such a thing possible? she exclaimed in surprise, remembering her own experiences, and the complete lack of any suggestion of a lifesong within these soulless entities.

I believe so. He leant forward, clutching her hands tightly in his intensity. *Think about it. Think of what it could mean. If these people could be returned to the light, perhaps the terrible sickness of self that has infested this planet for millennia could be lifted.*

Yes, she breathed, caught up in his vision. *They could be saved...*

We don't need saving! Her lover's voice, flat and angry, intruded into their shared moment. Almost annoyed she turned upon him.

But you do, she replied passionately. *You need saving from yourselves. Your entire world, this planet, you are killing it, slowly and terribly. It has been raped and mutilated until it can bear no more.*

That's a bit harsh, he retorted, yet she saw by the way his eyes would not meet her own, that he heard and recognised the truth in what she said.

Is it? Her father's calm voice defused the heat rising between them. *Is it not time to recognise the truth,* he continued, *to admit to what you have become?*

And what have we become? Her lover demanded hotly.

A race of self-obsessed and greed-driven beings. You consume without heed for consequence, you destroy that which you need to survive. A species that breeds without the need for conjoining...

Conjoining? her lover's voice was confused. Hastily she explained.

It is how children are conceived on my world. Children can only be born to couples who reach a level of complete loving harmony. The child must be wanted equally by both, or conception does not occur. It ensures that every child is loved and nurtured.

How very different on this world, her father remarked, his tone silky, bordering on sarcasm. *Where children are bred indiscriminately, born to lives of poverty, violence, and neglect. Yet, it was this ability to breed vast numbers of offspring which tipped the balance in your species' favour. That, and a ruthless, single-minded desire for self-advancement. Survival of the fittest, I believe you call it, but that is merely a term to hide what your species are...*

That's not true. It's just not true ... We're not... I mean...

Her father raised his head, regarding her lover steadily, until he looked away in shameful acknowledgement. Her heart moved by his miserable silence, she placed her cold hand over his, touched by the fleeting look of gratitude he shot her.

Tell me about your students, she urged her father, desperate to defuse the ominous, angry atmosphere which lay over them. *Tell me about your work.*

It has taken many years, but I have gathered around me those who perhaps, out of all the people on this world, have an inkling of what they have lost – a racial memory if you will – of what they once were. Together, we have chosen to remove ourselves from the toxin of this world. We study, meditate, and attempt to reach within ourselves to tap into the core of lifesong which I believe still lies buried, locked away, within each, and every, person.

And are you successful? she asked, intrigued by the vision his words created.

Sometimes, there is a spark, a glow. Some of my more advanced students report feeling a pulse, a rhythm. We have hope, and I feel the very act of trying to attain their lifesong may help the people of this planet to finally be at peace with themselves.

But you are merely one, she murmured. *How can you possibly hope to reach them all?*

This is but one of the sanctuaries I have created on this world, he told her, his voice touched with pride. *There are another seven led by my most promising students, I travel in turn to each. Fortunately, I happened to be in this place when you crossed over, possibly my presence acted as a beacon, calling you to me.*

Father! Once again, she clasped his hands in enthusiasm. *Now that I am here, I want to help you, help these people. I have seen the suffering and unrest that plagues them. I would like to assist you in your work, perhaps together...*

No.

Her father's flat refusal shocked and dismayed her. Hurt, she pulled her hands away from him and leaned back in her chair.

My daughter, I would wish nothing more than to spend my life with you and share my work, but you cannot stay here. Already, the scrap of lifesong I placed within you is diminishing, I am aware of this, even if you are not. Soon it will be gone, and then you will die. No, you must return.

It's impossible to return, she cried. *I tried so hard, but the link was gone.*

The link is still there, he reassured. *You were just unable to feel it. The sickness infecting this planet has numbed your ability. But hopefully, with my help, and with the combined efforts of my students, we may be able to send you home.*

Chapter Ten
The Journey

All was ready. She felt comforted by her father's confidence, but behind his eyes, she saw concern and was afraid.

She feared they would fail in the attempt, and her thin scrap of existence would be extinguished, snuffed out like the flame of a candle.

She feared in this desperate attempt to return her home, her father's remaining dregs of lifesong would be drained, and she feared his students – all those earnest, gentle souls who watched her with eyes of wonder and awe – would also somehow be harmed.

Her lover stayed close, his rock-like presence a source of strength and determination. Each time her eyes strayed to his, the truth moved between them. Succeed or fail, after this night they would be together no more.

When her father had declared his intention, and hurried away to alert his students to make their preparations, she had taken her lover by the hand and led him to the room she had awoken in.

Bolting the door, she had held him to her one last time, and their souls and essences had mingled in one final sublime joining, attaining a level of harmony never-before achieved, their cries of passionate relief merging into sorrow at the parting that was to come.

Now he stood beside her, a warm hand closed firmly over her icy fist, and his silent contemplation of the activity in the room somehow soothed and centred her.

A fire burnt on a large central hearth around which the students sat in a circle. Deep in meditation, their eyes were open, but they no longer saw.

Voices murmured together in a chant she recognised – it was the chapla – the calling to self of the great song.

The low, wordless tones set her heart beating with a fierce response, and she felt her pulse, shallow and uncertain now, peak with anticipation.

Softly, her father beckoned to her. It was time. She turned to her lover.

You have to go, he murmured. She nodded, unable to speak past the lump that threatened to choke her.

I promise, he began, emotion husking his voice, *I promise to try and make a difference, I will help your father. Perhaps the two of us can make a difference.*

She smiled and nodded again. He fell silent, holding onto her hand as if he would never let go. Behind them, her father cleared his throat. Reluctantly they released their hands and stepped apart.

Without words, they gazed at each other, filling their hearts and minds one last time. He touched her face gently, before turning her towards the circle, towards her father, and she knew he was of her past now. Resolutely, she squared her shoulders and moved to her father's side.

Holding out a hand, he dropped a bundle of herbs onto the fire and instantly, fumes – choking and all-consuming – snatched at her lungs, greedily sucking at her breath.

She gasped, afraid, then felt her father's grip on her shoulders. Firmly he held her over the smoke, and she inhaled deeply, the chanting of the students seeming to increase in pace and intensity.

She blinked … and was elsewhere … moving through time and space. She searched for the silver thread but could not see it.

Panic gripped, and she fought against the force which dragged her relentlessly on, terrified, wishing only to return to her father, and her lover.

Softly, child, softly…

The voice was everywhere and nowhere. It moved through and around her…

It was ancient and of now … it was all-powerful yet benevolent, and she relaxed, instinctively knowing it meant her no harm.

Who are you? she cried, or perhaps merely thought. *Where are you? What are you?*

Do you not recognise me? It demanded, and she felt the notes thrum through her blood and her bones, felt the pulse of life beat steady and true within her body, heard the rhythm pulse through the very fabric of existence.

The great song … she breathed, felt its glow of almost humour.

That is one of my names, it mused.

Tell me, show me! she demanded.

Ah, child, what would you know?

Everything! she cried recklessly, giddy with its presence.

So, it took her and showed her…

… whole universes moving ceaselessly within the inky blackness of space, planets throbbing to the beat of lifesong all worshipping the great song. She saw it in its many guises, all benign…

… saw whole worlds bathed in its light and she laughed aloud at its magnificence.

But there were other worlds from which no light came. Plunged into perpetual gloom, they were scattered and few, but she saw how potent their infection was.

Moving on, she saw her lover's world, a world she had come to care greatly for, crouching in its foul cloud of darkness.

What causes this? she cried, and it showed her. The Other. Insidious. Dark. Malicious.

A direct counterbalance to the great song, it crept amongst the stars searching for prey. Nameless, formless, it was mostly unsuccessful, but a few – a precious few – listened to its oily promises and made deals that condemned their species forever.

The great song whirled the dust of millennia, and she saw her lover's world as it had been. Teeming with lifesong, all species existing in perfect harmony; all equal in the eyes of one another.

She saw the darkness reach the young world, its subtle searching of their souls, the filthy bargain that was struck.

Paradise was lost.

Their lifesongs were suppressed forever, the darkness fed off its power, and, in exchange, their race became consumed with the urge to survive and triumph at any cost.

She saw the need for conjoining overcome; the hordes of children bred to swarm like a virus over the surface of the planet.

She saw other species exploited for want and need. She even saw the other humanoid races which shared their world hunted into extinction.

One race hung on for longer than the others, heavy of brow yet pure of lifesong. They fled further and further from the new violence of her lover's race, but it was no use.

The planet was no longer big enough to contain the two species.

Crying out in grief and horror, she looked away and the great song whirled her through time. She was comforted by the sight of millions of worlds flooded with its pure, blinding light.

But the darkness was always there, waiting, ready to spread its message of greed and hate.

You must be strong, child, the great song murmured through her bones. *Much depends on you.*

The subtle yet persistent pressure suddenly ceased. For a moment, she was floating over the chamber where students chanted, and a fire burned.

She saw a shadow of her body begin to solidify in her father's arms.

No!

She felt him cry out and saw the herbs he desperately threw onto the fire. The increased vigour of the chanting hurled her back once more, jerking upwards and away from her lover's world, then floating, uncertain and afraid.

The darkness was absolute, the only relief a thin, so thin, strand of silver thread stretching away into the distance.

She followed it, heart pounding in an all-consuming fear, until suddenly it ended, fading into nothing.

She stopped, lost and alone in the silence, abandoned by all, unable even to hear the great song.

Help me!

She screamed aloud, twisting in the darkness. Too afraid to go on and unable to go back, stranded between worlds, her strength failing, her lifesong withering and dying.

Wait, what was this?

An echo.

A melody.

Subtle yet insistent, it pulsed through the darkness.

Gratefully she felt for it, feeling it grow stronger in its intensity the more she moved towards it.

Throbbing through her heart and brain, it spoke of home, of safety and love.

Joyfully, she slid along it and, in a burst of light, saw her room on her world.

Her body, pale and wraith-like, lying upon the bed, and, surrounding it, a solid circle of the Council of Elders, their lifesongs reaching into the darkness, pulling her to them, dragging her home.

Gasping in shock, she landed with a thud inside her body and opened her eyes to the relieved steady gaze of the Wise One.

"Welcome back," he said.

For the first three days after her return, she slept the sleep of the dead, only awakening to consume vast quantities of food, her malnourished body desperate to reclaim all it had lost.

And, on the fourth day, they took her to see her father. Leading her deeper and deeper into the furthermost reaches of the caves sacred to the Council of Elders, she felt the power of the lifesong oozing from its walls, realising the sanctity and strength of the place.

Finally, they reached the deepest cavern, and there – surrounded by a circle of chanting elders – lay her father.

Wonderingly, she approached, knelt by his side, and gently touched his translucent skin, stroking his barely-there hair.

"We did not know if we were helping at all," one murmured to her. "Maintaining his body, feeding his soul with constant lifesong. We were too late to save your mother, but we hoped that maybe, we were helping in some small way..."

"You are," she reassured them. "Oh, believe me, you are."

Much had been spoken of in the months since her return. The Council of Elders had listened and questioned until every single morsel of information had been extracted from her experience.

Their countenances darkened at her story of the infection which had claimed the lifesongs of other worlds.

As she told of all that the great song had shown her, had told her, they exchanged glances of deepest despair.

Finally, she returned to her home, to her quiet, simple life, moving through her days and months much as before. Yet, all was different now.

The Wise One came to see her. After the usual niceties of greeting and the ritual of tea had been observed, he sat with her on the bench outside the dwelling, watching the sunset over the sea.

"It has been decided to tell the people nothing of this,'" he declared.

She was silent, waiting for him to continue.

"After all, this other world is so far away, it will take millennia before they could reach us with these ships of space you spoke of. By then, who knows, maybe a cure will have been found against the infection they carry."

"Maybe," she agreed quietly.

After he had gone, as she held her baby close to her breast and gazed into the bright alien blueness of his eyes, she thought of her lover's world ... of its people, of their drive and determination, of the unceasing, always present need that spurred his race to forever strive for more and more.

Somehow, she did not believe they would have that long...

The End

~ About the Author ~

Julia Blake lives in the beautiful historical town of Bury St. Edmunds, in the county of Suffolk in the UK, with her daughter, one crazy cat, and a succession of even crazier lodgers.

Her first novel, The Book of Eve, met with worldwide critical acclaim, and since then, Julia has released ten other books which have delighted her growing number of readers with their strong plots and instantly relatable characters. Details of all Julia's novels can be found on the next page.

Julia leads a busy life, juggling work, and family commitments with her writing, and has a strong internet presence, loving the close-knit and supportive community of fellow authors she has found on social media. She promises there are plenty more books in the pipeline.

Julia says: "I write the kind of books I like to read myself, warm and engaging novels, with strong, three-dimensional characters you can connect with."

~ A Note from Julia ~

If you have enjoyed this book, why not take a few moments to leave a review on Amazon,

It needn't be much, just a few lines saying you liked the book and why, yet it can make a world of difference.

Reviews are the reader's way of letting the author know they enjoyed their book, and of letting other readers know the book is an enjoyable read and why. It also informs Amazon that this is a book worth promoting, and the more reviews a book receives, the more Amazon will recommend it to other readers.

I would be very grateful and would like to say thank you for reading my book and if you do spare a few minutes of your time to review it, I do see, read, and appreciate every single review left for me.

Best Regards
Julia Blake

~ Other Books by the Author ~

Black Ice

An exciting steampunk retelling of the
Snow White fairy tale

The Forest ~ a tale of old magic ~

Myth, folklore, and magic combine in this engrossing
tale of a forgotten village and an ancient curse

Erinsmore

A wonderful tale of an enchanted land of sword and sorcery, myth and magic, dragons, and prophecy

The Book of Eve

A story of love, betrayal, and bitter secrets that threaten to rip a young woman's life apart

The Perennials Series

Becoming Lili – the beautiful, coming of age saga
Chaining Daisy – its gripping sequel
Rambling Rose – the triumphant conclusion

The Blackwood Family Saga

Fast-paced and heart-warming, this exciting series
tells the story of the Blackwood Family and their
search for love and happiness

Eclairs for Tea and Other Stories

A fun collection of short stories and quirky poems
that reflect the author's multi-genre versatility

.

Printed in Great Britain
by Amazon